A
BY
DAWESY
BOOK!

— TALES OF A — *whisper*

THE GOBLIN LADY

Written & Created by

OLIVER DAWES

ISBN 978-1-5272-3290-7

First published in the UK 2018

www.bydawesy.com

Illustrations by James Willetts

Printed and bound in the UK

A pocket full of pets

I remember her so clearly, as if she were stood in the room with us now, and the smell … well, I don't know if you've ever smelled a badger's bum mixed with the ripest crisp green leaves? It's an odd mix for sure – both unpleasant and bearable at the same time (thanks to the fresh leaves).

I was scared of her at first, most children were. We didn't really understand.

It's sad how sometimes the most innocent, honest and introverted people – due to their vulnerability – can be seen as backwards, when in fact they probably understand more than we could ever wish to. Everybody deserves a chance to be understood.

I was just six years old when I first laid eyes on her. We were having a family picnic and Mr Albert Sausage – our sausage dog – had stolen a cake from the picnic. He went charging off into the hedges, his little chunky sausage legs moving slower than his brain intended; I thought it was hilarious so I started chasing him. As I got closer to the hedges, that smell hit me – badger's bum and fresh green leaves! I looked up and there she was, just standing there behind the foliage: wiry, wavy hair with a bird's nest neatly resting in her un-brushed tangles, and bird poop seeping down one side of her head!

She wore a large olive-green overcoat covering most of her disproportionate frame – thin gangly arms and legs with a bloated midriff – as if it was made for her. It complimented her imperfections. Baby animals sat in her pockets; they seemed comfortable – all snug as a bug in an olive-green rug. I remember seeing a rabbit and a baby fox, very odd indeed! But they seemed calm.

I had only ever heard about her before: people would say they didn't know where she came from. But it was her right to live where she wanted … so left alone in the woods, she was.

Her face … it looked like she hadn't washed for years: three teeth I counted when she smiled at me, three yellowish stumps! More warts than you could shake a stick at and a high-pitched excitable voice.

She smiled at me and said, "do you want to feed my worms?" At this point Albert Sausage barked and ran away, but I stayed – not by choice, I was mesmerised for a moment, pinned to the spot.

After a few moments, I snapped out of my daze, gasped and started to run away – she then scuttled off in the opposite direction giggling and shouting, "worms need breakfast too you know! Feeeed the worms, feed them good and proper!" Her voice echoed through the woods as she scuttled away.

I stopped halfway, running back towards my picnic, looked back and she was gone! But I was no longer scared – I thought she was misunderstood, and I felt that way at just six years old; she wasn't that scary really, just never given a chance to be accepted.

It was only a couple of years later, when I was eight years old, sat in class at my primary school – Lakeside Hills Primary – that her origins and secrecy finally started to unravel …

"So, does anybody know what's happening this weekend here in Lakeside?" said Mrs Angel, my teacher.

I liked Mrs Angel. As her name suggested, she was rather patient and kind – always glowing and smiling. She had a soft voice, but her class could be testing at times – especially today. "Oh, oh, I know –" said Kevin "aliens are landing?" The class chuckled "– big fat green zombie aliens!"

This was a typical comment from Kevin – the class clown – always sat there so confident and sure of himself; I mean he was a big kid, almost twice the size of most of us eight year olds. He would sometimes pick fights with children in the year above, and win! Kevin had thick ginger curly locks and was heavily freckled; his constant chewing of a pen – rather than using it for academic purposes – meant he usually had ink stains in the corners of his mouth, which reminded me of a feral dog.

"Shush now class; any serious answers?" Mrs Angel responded.

"My daddy said the bulldozers are coming – to pull down the woods!"

"Correct Lacey, your daddy is right, and so are you."

I was in love with Lacey, in fact I called her Lacey Love, only to myself of course … oh and to the pictures I drew of her in crayon on the inside of my bedroom door – I created a Lacey shrine; luckily, I could never become embarrassed if anyone discovered my drawings as they were so bad. The last person that saw the pictures said, "oh wow you must sure like lemon lollypops, you have drawn a lot of them!" Of course, I agreed to them being lollypops even if I was a little insulted. I would just say "hey, they're pineapple lollypops!"

Lacey had beautiful long blonde hair and the cutest little glasses; ahhhhh Lacey Love, how I would often stare across class, and you would catch me in a trance …

Mrs Angel continued – "Now I know we worked together as a community as best as we could to stop this from happening, but unfortunately new houses are being built, and I wanted to remind you all to stay well away from the building site."

"But what about the animals Mrs Angel?" said Henry.

"I'm sure they'll run away and find a safe new home."

I could see Mrs Angel wasn't completely convinced by her loose answer of the animals' genuine safety; her good heart clearly carried some concern.

Henry was top of the class – a nerd I suppose – a good kid; we hung out now and then. Kevin – the class bully – used to pay Henry to do his homework. He would pay him in chocolate bars, even though everyone knew Kevin stole those chocolate bars from other children's lunch boxes – but you couldn't deny the trade: chocolate for homework or else Kevin would perform his special wrestling move on you, which meant spinning you round by your arms in the playground – then he would try tossing you into the trash whilst shouting "Kevin shoots, he scores!" as you were thrown through the air: what a mean boy! And, to add insult to injury, nine times out of ten Kevin would end up stealing half the chocolate back off you.

Anyway, back to the class – at this point, without thinking how my classmates would react, I shouted out …

"What about The Lady?"

This was the first time it occurred to me that she may not be safe staying in the woods anymore.

"How about what Lady?" said Mrs Angel.
"The one … the one in the woods," I stuttered, "where will she go?"
"You mean The Goblin Lady!" Kevin shouted. The class chuckled again, everyone started doing their best goblin impressions.
"Enough Kevin, and everyone else, you know we don't talk about The Lady in the woods."
"But she's kind! I've seen her!" I shouted. The class gasped, some in shock.
"What do you mean you've seen her Ivor? Do your parents know about this?"

"No – I did honest, she looks after the animals, and she doesn't seem like a goblin."
"Ivor, we don't talk about The Gob... The Lady" Mrs Angel said, stopping herself from saying goblin.
Suddenly the class started chanting "Goblin! Goblin! Goblin!" over and over.

I was so upset. People just didn't want to understand that this wasn't a goblin, this was a human being like you and me; just someone who didn't follow the crowd – someone who was living their life, their way, which made them happy and feel free.

I stood on my desk and shouted!

"Stop, I will find her, and I will show you all she has a kind heart!"
"Get down Mr Neverstump or I'll call your parents immediately!" yelled Mrs Angel.
The chanting was still going on, but I stood strong; well that was until the leg on my desk snapped and I fell off ... everyone started laughing, then the bell went – that just about saved my embarrassment.

But this was truly the moment my protest to save The Goblin Lady from the bulldozers began.

Kevin passed me on the floor laughing and uttered "good work Neverstump – at least I now know not to stand on a desk, especially if it collapses under your scrawny legs."
Everyone left class; I looked up and Mrs Angel was standing over me with crossed arms, tapping her foot.

"I think we need a little talk after school young man, don't you ...?"

Albert Sausage – a knight's horse

I had that little talk after school – Mrs Angel even called my parents in. They said I had mentioned that I had seen The Lady once, but they just put it down to my active imagination; that's what they always said to me: "Ivor, that imagination of yours will get you into trouble!"

Crazy thing was, they also knew she was in the woods: they'd lived in Lakeside for 30 years. People were in denial about her, some were even scared. In the past, you would have heard whispers that she was a witch, but the whispers had stopped. People had realised – quite simply – that Lakeside Hills was a beautiful place; a beautiful place with odd goings on and strange things happening throughout the years, yes, but never any major trouble. No awful crimes and certainly no evil; so the whispers had disappeared because people had decided she couldn't be a witch.

Humans can become mean when they don't understand something; they either pretend it doesn't exist, or focus on the fact it doesn't look that pretty – so, 'The Goblin Lady' was who she became known as; or at least to those that bothered to accept her existence at all.

There were the select few who would just call her The Lady, missing out the Goblin part – trying to show her at least an ounce of respect. And finally, there were those who were terrified of her – and that fear would then run throughout whole families, whispers of dark and sinister tales …

That night when mum and dad went to sleep, I knew I needed to find her and let her know what was happening to our local woodland area; I guess I've always carried a sense of intrigue and adventure, so my parents were partly correct about that.

I laid in bed looking up at the ceiling for hours, waiting for mum and dad to go to bed.

There was a poster on the ceiling above my bed and it read "you will never have a completely bad day if you show kindness at least once." – a poster my nanna got me: she was a very wise lady. The more I stared at it, the more determined I got to go out and find her that night!

It felt like days, but it must have only been a couple of hours before I finally heard my parents come upstairs and close their door. I looked around my room for something to wear – usually I would just stick on any old gear but not tonight; tonight, I was on a mission – an adventure! Would I finally make proper contact with her?

I found some old combat trousers I used for cub scouts, a superhero cartoon jumper, a head torch, an old duvet cover I used as a cape; I gathered some biscuits in a napkin and armed myself with my plastic toy sword and knight's battle helmet (in case things got a little heated).

At the time I felt good – I felt powerful – but I probably looked ridiculous: would soft plastic battle objects save me against a possible goblin?

I remember looking out my window and it was a long way down … I thought to myself – this kind of thing seems easier in the movies, so I decided to go downstairs instead.

As I crept through the house, Albert Sausage (my dog) started pulling at my cape!

"No Albert," I whisper shouted – have you ever done a whisper shout? Try it, it's quite fun, you have to yell as loud as you can but under your breath! It's hard to get your point across when you need to be silent –
"Sausage no!" I kept whisper shouting.

Albert Sausage was just growling in a playful manner, tail wagging and pulling at my cape; he almost gave the game away that I was out of bed.

By the time I got to the front door I figured Albert Sausage was coming with me. If I left him now he'd just start barking and wake the house – besides, he was always my wingman! He'd keep me safe. So off I marched into the night … armed with plastic sword and plastic knight's helmet – alongside my powerful knight's horse: Albert Sausage!

Well … I mean, I felt like a knight with a horse, but Albert couldn't carry his own fat legs half the time, let alone me on his back! So instead we walked side by side, Albert Sausage now carrying my makeshift cape in his mouth dragging it through the mud and grass. What a pathetic pair of superhero knights we must have looked … but what is more important than the way you look? Bravery, enthusiasm, heart and optimism! And between us both, I was sure we could conjure up a handful of those characteristics – at least for the time being anyway.

Mummy cuddles

People used to say – to find her, follow her high-pitched voice, she would be casting spells and turning children into baby animals, so she could keep them in her pockets. And if you can't hear her, follow that smell … badger's bum and fresh green leaves! I found it hard to believe she could turn children into baby animals; at least that's what I had to keep telling myself!

It was dark, very dark; the woods were outside of the street lamps' range and all I had was the small orange glow that came from my cheap children's head torch; it created a laughably small visual on the floor which couldn't have been much bigger than a dinner plate! Built for fun not for action quite clearly – or not so clearly as it happens … but it was enough light to get us by for now.

We eventually reached the woods: Albert Sausage and me, finally about to find and help The Lady.

Either that or be gobbled up and never seen again, but NO! – I kept reminding myself, I could sense her kindness and there was no way I would let her be potentially crushed by a bulldozer while she slept: do goblins even sleep I thought to myself? *She's not a goblin* I swiftly reminded myself once again!

As we edged further and further into the woods my head torch started to dim – "oh no! I didn't pack spare batteries" I whispered to Albert. But as my concern for the creeping darkness increased, I realised my search might end sooner than anticipated – there it was … the smell of badger's bum and fresh green leaves. I couldn't believe it, I was finally going to see her again!

But that wasn't to be the case; when I looked a few yards in front of me, what I saw was a badger eating some fresh green leaves, stood next to what looked like its latest deposit … yuck! I groaned about that smell quite loudly and the badger was spooked, rose up on its hind legs – let out a mighty scream and ran into the bushes. That was far too much fear and excitement for me and Albert, so we ran quickly in the other direction. Surely we had made too much noise? Had she heard us? Could I protect Albert and myself armed with only a plastic helmet and sword? I was now shaking with confusion; "what are we doing Albert?" I whispered. "Maybe we should go home?" Now I was even questioning if I ever had seen her? Had I really seen her that day? Or had I been imagining things like my parents said to Mrs Angel? If you tell someone something enough, they'll start to believe it. Was my imagination taking over? Were the smells people talked about just a smelly old badger eating its dinner in the woods – and it's a rumour that's got out of hand? Is a badger The Goblin Lady? Oh my, that must be it! The Goblin Lady is a badger! I smiled and laughed to myself dishonestly; "well that must be it then Albert, all this time that Goblin Lady was just a smelly old badger!"

As I stepped backwards whilst looking forwards into the darkness checking no one was there or following us, I lost my balance and I fell back into what seemed like a pit – I screamed and Albert barked! I felt myself crash into a huge pile of leaves after rolling for a few moments down a small steep hill … then suddenly … BUMP! And darkness – I had passed out, hit my head maybe? But what I awoke to, I'll never forget.

"Ah ha ha ha!" a squeaky high-pitched cackle echoed as I awoke – was I in some kind of small hut?

And there she was … I was a bit groggy, where was Albert, I thought?

"Hello?" I said. "Is it you?"

There she was, so content and happy – bouncing around her kitchen area like she'd eaten far too many candy apples!?

"You're awake! I've made you a broth," she said, "a lovely beautiful broth, fit for a boy – a boy to grow big and strong – a boy that can help all the creatures in the world and spread kindness throughout the animal kingdom."

To begin with I didn't know what to make of her character! She was buzzing – full of energy – but I felt like she could turn, like she was on edge. I think it was the squeaky loud high-pitched voice that threw me; had she just spoken normally I would have felt more at ease, but I had to keep reminding myself I trusted my intuition that she was good person – her energy just made me feel uneasy initially.

I didn't really reply to her offering of broth; I was more shocked that I had actually found her, and where was Albert I thought? I had also lost my plastic knight's sword and helmet in the fall, not that it would have helped me. I sat silent for a moment mesmerised, watching her move around – she was like a spider – a bloated midriff with long hairy arms and legs, making the most unpredictable movements.

"Where am I? Where is Albert?" I asked.

She sat down in front of me rather heavily and in a heap, like dropping a sack of potatoes; her disproportionate body of long gangly arms and legs bounced upwards as her bloated midriff hit the floor in an animated fashion – she spilled the broth all down her dirty long green jacket upon impact with the ground.

"Oh, fiddle flumps!" she said, "look at the mess I've made? Oh well I can always whip you up another broth – it's really easy! It's tree bark, heaven sent beetle wings, dandelion stalk juice and some of my tears for good measure – and do you know how I extract my tears? I just look outside at all those poor lonely animals and that's it … I cry, I can't help it! I just love them all so much."

"No, no, it's fine," I said, "I'm not hungry."

"I'm sorry, I'm getting far too carried away, aren't I? I've just not had company in a while and already half of you has left; it ran off once you fell into my front garden – that beautiful fat fluffy baby you had with you, I think I spooked it when I ran towards it shouting MUMMY CUDDLES, GIVE MUMMY THOSE BIG FLAPPY EARS! Maybe I should have introduced myself first?"

"What Albert ran away?" I replied.

I was relieved by the fact Albert was usually good at finding his way home, but this wasn't good, not good at all, I hoped he was safe.

"Look …" The Lady said, "I don't know what you're doing here, but you fell into my underground cabin; those leaves covered the entrance to my door and you fell right down here and banged your little nugget on my front door! I'd arranged those leaves lovely yesterday and you went and spoiled them – that's my front garden that is."

"I'm sorry," I said anxiously.

"Not to worry, not to worry … now what's a boy of your age doing in the woods at this time? You can't stay here long – you know they're coming, don't you? We have to do something! I've been preparing." she said flexing her thin and tiny arm muscles.

"Who are you talking about?"

"The men – they wear those bright yellow vests, brighter than the sun. And have giant half acorns on their nuggets; those big fat stinky men that eat all those horrible breakfasts made from liquefied pig's eyes and snouts."

"Sausages you mean?" I replied.

"And they eat the insides of shells that come from a bird's bum." Now The Lady began to rant.

"Eggs?"

"Yeah that's the stuff, why do they do that? It's got babies in it!"

"Umm, I don't know, it's a cooked breakfast I think, I've had them before, my mum makes them for me sometimes."

"What ever happened to good old Dry Leaf Flakes? That's what people should be having, much better for your teeth; I've been here a long time you know, my memory of my old life is shabby – I remember most things, but I think I've learned a new way of life here – a pure life; I've blocked out many bad memories, things I no longer believe in, but I still remember … I still remember some things."

As she smiled there were leaves stuck in her teeth from what looked like weeks ago; she opened a cabinet which contained around twenty boxes of Dry Leaf Flakes. I'd never even seen or heard of people eating dried leaves, let alone them being manufactured and having their own boxes; where on earth did she get them from I thought?

"Why do you have so many boxes of dried leaves?"

"That's just today's supply, I'm running low! Do you want some?"

Before I could even answer she began to pour them on my head in an excitable uncontrollable manner.

"I've forgotten a bowl, how rude of me," she shouted – spinning around to grab one, knocking a few items to the floor, some of them smashing. The etiquette of her pouring Dry Leaf Flakes on my head – not being considered as the rude part of her kind gesture – did make me giggle … if only a little: I still wasn't completely at ease.

"I make these myself! And the boxes – all natural, all good for your bones," she said excitedly, as if she were pitching a new product to an investor. It was at the this point I realised she was quite scatty in her mannerisms and energy – the way she spoke, bouncing from one thing to the other without even taking a breath – the way she moved, almost gracefully and effortlessly – yet as if she had a pogo stick attached to her legs: it all reminded me of a kitten playing with a toy mouse but continuously keeping the mouse in the air, panicking if the mouse had the slightest chance of touching the floor.

"No stop!" I said trying to calm her energy. I was still trying to make sense of everything since I entered her cabin. "Wait! How do you know about these men? Who are they? What do they want?"

Suddenly her energy went from one hundred miles per hour to zero.

"Come with me." she whispered. She led me to a room in her cabin; for a moment she finally descended into calm – which was very welcome at this point – but what was she about to show me I thought?

Three kind mice

We were walking through a chamber towards a door – the chamber was dark and dimly lit by flickering candles up high which was useful considering my head torch had all but died by now. I could see the light at the end of the chamber pushing through the gaps in the door; it reminded me of the gates of heaven mother would describe to me – a blinding light pushing through the clouds. As we got closer I heard chirping, purring and rustling – so many sounds, so much activity!

As we arrived at the door, The Lady grabbed an old smelly baseball cap from her large olive-green coat pocket. "Put this on," she said.
"Why?" I asked?
"You'll see ..."

Reluctantly, I placed it on my head after sniffing it and feeling disgusted at the stench and stains. She swung the door open and my jaw dropped ... hundreds of small animals everywhere – many moving around freely and happily – all in harmony; no predators chasing prey, it was unreal, like a real-life cartoon.

There were animals on what looked like mini hospital beds, some walking around with bandages on! It was like an extremely busy hospital treatment room. There was a variety of birds, mice, foxes, badgers, hedgehogs and some animals I didn't even recognise. Some wearing the most adorable outfits; I could see she had made them herself as there was a sewing machine in one corner with materials attached.

Now I knew why I wore the cap, to stop the birds pooping on my head – not that The Lady minded, she already had what looked like a bird's nest in her wiry wavy hair, with poop dripping down one side of her cheek! I guess the dirty hat was a gesture of some hospitality on her part, *at least she tried* I thought.

"What is this place?" I asked.
"I am the nurse of these woods; I take in poorly animals and make them better."
"Wow" I said.

I was shocked. You could see she had tended to so many sick animals and shown them so much love – they wouldn't even fight amongst one another.

But what was even more amazing is they were listening to her – in a form of body language. Plus she would mimic the sounds of the animals, it was truly amazing. They eventually settled down once she explained to them I meant no harm – they were part panicked, part excited by my presence – I realised I was her first visitor in a very long time, but she trusted me as I was only a lost child.

Towards the back of the room was a wall filled with newspapers and plans; it wasn't the animals she wanted to show me (although to the average person, the sight was bizarre) – to her this was clearly all so normal. She pointed to the newspapers on the wall; it seemed one of the local paper boys had been dumping papers in the woods and she had got hold of them, finding out the intention to build houses where the woods were.

A tear rolled down her face as she pointed to the newspapers, you could see the sadness in her face. What was extraordinary was the plans next to the newspapers were all drawn out, featuring herself and the animals – she had designed these plans; they were plans that she had made to sabotage the workers and stop the build from happening. I saw it all, so clear, right in front of me, I wasn't saving her from the bulldozers after all; she was saving the community and the animals from something hardly anybody wanted: she had been planning this for months!

I told her – this is what I came to find you about, and you're already prepared! A bird landed on her outreached hand, she kissed it on the beak and it flew off again. She told me she remembered me – she remembered seeing me a couple of years ago, she saw a kindness in me and knew we would meet again; she was pleased I had come to find her; not many people believed she existed or ever saw her, but that's how she liked it really. We had an instant connection. The Lady respected my courageous effort to warn her of the new danger – putting myself at risk in the process, wandering so late at night, so she opened up to me.

"Would you like to know more about me?" she asked.
"Yes please." I said.
The excitement in her voice picked up again and she shouted – "STORY TIME! STORY TIME! GET YOUR SNACKS, SEEDS, NUTS AND DRY LEAF FLAKES!"

She was clapping her hands and bouncing up and down; all the animals gathered round like a bunch of primary school children and sat to listen. The respect, communication and bond between them all was incredible – they were like a huge family. This wasn't something that had developed overnight, this was years of trust.

I sat down and three mice sat on my shoulders; they were so human-like in their mannerisms – one of them crossed its little legs and leaned on my neck with their arm to get comfortable – I gulped! I had never been this close to mice before, certainly not ones like this.

The Lady began to speak …

Story time

"I know what they call me ... they call me The Goblin Lady.

But that's not my name, I was born Margaret ... Margaret Weathersby.

Not that anyone knows me as that anymore, I don't even receive mail with my name on, and if I ever need anything via birdy airmail I ask Doris to grab it for me." She nodded at Doris the magpie, who let out a tweet in response.

"I used to be known in Lakeside – pretty well known; I had friends, family, a job; but everything I need is here now, this is my family. I've lived in these woods for almost twenty years and NOW they want to take it away? – we won't let them.

I once owned the only pet shop in Lakeside, a lovely little shop it was. We provided food, toys, small pet cages, custom pet housing and – importantly – minor injury care. In my shop I had regulars, friends, people would come in with their beautiful pets and we would talk for hours, it was my dream job, it really was.

I was married to the chairman of a large pet food company. One day, my husband came home and told me they were opening a new store not far from Lakeside Hills which would undercut my prices and services drastically – *you'll have to close!* he said. *But don't worry, it's a very healthy deal and we will be well-off financially; you can stay at home and not work.*

I could wait on him twenty-four seven, he said to me – washing, ironing, every meal cooked on time.

WELL, I DON'T THINK SO YOU BIG FAT HAIRY …" she shouted! In that moment she went from calm story teller and back to her abrupt scatty nature – as this memory clearly still upset her. What I remember – but at the time put down to the wind outside – was upon her outburst the whole cabin shook, but the animals stayed calm, very bizarre indeed!? Once composed she continued with her story …

"Who did he think I was? That wasn't my purpose in life! *I'm to be with the animals* I told him! *Why would you want to work again?* he said back to me. But working with the animals was what I always wanted – I was completely devastated.

He offered me to work in the warehouse, there would be no customer interaction, no animal visits and the most rewarding part would be lost – no animal injury care. I would just be slogging twenty-kilogram bags of food all day! *NO NO NO* I said to him, *this is not me.*

Months later I had lost too many customers. Some stayed loyal, but others were charmed by huge discounts I just couldn't offer. I was so sad, but he didn't sympathise, and I couldn't go to him for comfort.

He then became so busy with all the new pet stores nationally that I hardly saw him anymore; I would have chosen a cute little pet store and being able to get by with the love of my husband being around over having more money, never seeing him and no emotional investment.

People used to bring injured strays from the woods to my shop to care for; we received a small budget from the council to treat them then release them back into the wild. Now – with the new superstore open and further away – people were leaving more strays to suffer: the trip was too far and too inconvenient.

I used to take walks through the woods when I was sad and find so many injured or sick animals, it often became overwhelming; I even found a litter of puppies abandoned under a tree stump once.

One day I had enough! I began to make a small cabin in the woods to help some of the animals; I built it away from the street where I could work in peace without being questioned or judged. The cabin contained a small amount of medical supplies inside, but – being exposed – it soon got vandalised.

After not seeing my husband for weeks, I decided enough was enough: I took all my savings from my account and spent them on medical supplies and a basic ration of food and water – enough to last me years. I spent the next few months building an underground bunker in the woods using the money my husband transferred to me to keep me sweet: bribed into being a good little housewife.

Finally, it was done; I was ready to move into the bunker! I left my husband an honest note about how I hadn't been happy for almost a year and that he never listened to me when I was upset; I told him I was leaving – for good. It was the greatest most rewarding and peaceful decision I ever made. I spent so much time with the animals and away from modern entertainment systems that I started to learn animal vocal and body language. Years went by and I ran out of supplies, but my communication was now strong with the animals – we would organise trips to supermarket skips that would throw away out-of-date food and other damaged goods we could use to get by: the food was always ok for a few more days. I've only had food poisoning eighty-seven times and I'm still here!

So here we are 20 years on and I find out, due to a naughty young boy dumping newspapers in the woods, they're building these houses with no consideration for the wildlife; and that's why we put our heads together and came up with the plans to stop them!

On the wall in front of us are plans devised to stop the bulldozers getting us from any direction; we have two hundred and ninety-two possible outcomes! I mean … we have quite a lot of time on our hands down here – plus the badgers are mega indecisive and enjoy pinpoint planning accuracy. But as you can see, we're ready! The woods will forever be ours!"

The animals all cheered.

A boy is missing

Everything was so clear to me now – who she was, what she was about. I felt safe – we spent so much time talking that I hadn't realised I had been gone for almost twenty-four hours!?

We had sat chatting, explaining more and more about ourselves, both fascinated by each other's lives. Hours earlier we had sent out a spy fox and his two spy mice companions – they were dressed in face masks and capes to hide their identities, they looked adorable! I had asked The Lady to translate to the mice: to firstly see if the bulldozers were on their way, and, secondly – how the people I knew back home were reacting to me being missing – my parents, friends, teachers and the locals.

The fox and mice came back zipping through the woods, the mice riding the fox like two fearless jockeys on a racehorse! They unsaddled and came into the bunker in a panic …

The Lady had to translate for me – "It's not good," she said "the village is out of control, people are frightened, a boy is missing! The Goblin Lady is being blamed – I am being blamed? Your parents are searching frantically for you; they think you were taken from your bedroom. Albert Sausage is trying desperately in his doggy language to direct them here, but they don't understand him; most of what Albert is trying to say/bark is complaining about the brand of dog food your parents are using – but that's a complaint for another time. Albert also talks about you – well he barks about you! But they just don't understand him. A girl named Lacey pines for you; she is telling the other children she is sad. A boy called Henry believes he knows where you may have gone; he doesn't think you were taken – he is telling people you are too brave and courageous to let that happen. A mean boy called Kevin is telling Henry he is wrong, and you have been gobbled up by … by me!? A teacher is concerned, she says she should have listened to you – she thinks she could have helped you, advised or stopped you? One or the other, but it's not clear.

There is a situation … the bulldozers can no longer crash through the woods until you are found. But people are sad, a boy is missing … you can't stay here – you must go!"

It was at that moment I realised I should leave – especially if I was making people I cared about back home upset. I never meant to be gone as long as I had; I started to think … what would I say? I couldn't tell them about The Lady – they would blame her for my disappearance. I was so torn – would she be ok? Would her plans work …? By returning to the village it meant the bulldozers would begin to demolish the woods.

I decided firstly to make my way home, let everyone know I was ok, and then plan from there – so many thoughts going through my head. Two mice guided me out of the woods, they sat on my shoulder pointing which way I should walk; I had already become so attached to the amazing animals, they were a welcome pair on my journey home.

As I walked through the woods, I could see and hear people in the distance – they were calling my name; people were actually out looking for me … this was so bizarre.

I decided to keep down low and snuck my way through the bushes; suddenly I heard a surprised yelp "IVOR!" It was Lacey and Henry! They had found me! "Shhh!" I hissed at them. They were so excited – it took a few moments to calm them down – but when they did, we sat under an old tree stump nearby out of sight. The mice had run off by now … I had told the mice I would be ok, and they should go before my friends caught sight of them and didn't understand or became scared.

"I was so worried about you," said Lacey. "We thought … well, we thought –"
"I knew you would be ok," Henry piped up, stopping Lacey from saying she thought I was a goner!
"We have to get you back," Lacey said. "We have to let everyone know you're safe!"

I then proceeded to tell them what had happened and why I was here … they both looked shocked, but impressed, but mainly shocked.

"You saw her?" Henry said. "You really did? I can't believe it!"

For the next half an hour I was bombarded with questions, disbelief and excitement from both Lacey and Henry. Their excitement didn't come in the manner that this was the end and I was found – it was the fact that – from what I told them – this was just the beginning, and the battle of the bulldozers had just begun …

Sling shots and cups of tea

As we walked back towards the village –
through the woods – cautiously avoiding
anyone looking for me; I decided the best place
to lay low for a while was in Henry's attic. It
was like a kind of hideout that his parents
allowed him to go to; it was a really cool space!
He had a sofa, posters of his favourite super
heroes, a fridge with snacks in, computer
games and loads of other cool fun stuff; it was
any kid's dream hideout! The best part was –
because Henry was a smart kid – he was
allowed to do *mostly* what he liked as his
parents trusted him, and therefore we wouldn't
be disturbed.

When I look back now, it's like Henry was the
only kid I ever knew that played the growing
up game truly right! Do your work both at
home and in school, respect your parents and
be polite; just by following these simple rules,
he earned enough respect to be given the key to
freedom, mess those things up and he would be
grounded and lose it all.

But then again, it wasn't complete freedom, it was about living within boundaries and being smart about your moves – knowing right from wrong and reaping the benefits. I could have learned a lot from him back then if my brain wasn't always so preoccupied with strange goings on.

As we made our way to Henry's house, he and Lacey filled me in on what had happened over the past twenty-four hours …

My parents had gone out of their minds – I knew I really should go and tell them I was safe, but I needed both Henry and Lacey on my side first with a plan of action – in fact, during this whole Goblin Lady ordeal, or at least since I had left my bedroom that night, I really didn't see or hear from my parents at all; mainly because the only place they could ideally be was at home as per the advice given by authorities. It was the best place to be – should I be found – even if my father's natural instinct was to go looking himself; the whole village was already out looking for me! So, at home they awaited ANY news *or* my return … so I heard, anyway.

My parents had started to blame the school, as they believed there was an uncontrolled situation where the children were allowed to speak about The Goblin Lady; they thought such nonsense should have been banned to keep us safe. Mrs Angel was forced to feel partly responsible, and the headmaster gave her a telling off; his name was Mr Francis – apparently, he was so spooked by The Goblin Lady circumstances, that he felt a pressure to blame Mrs Angel when it was never her fault I went missing.

"Children get carried away, it's what they do; we can't stop their *tales of a whisper*." Mrs Angel told them. "It's this imagination that makes being a child so special."

During the mass panic of my mysterious disappearance, the school was temporarily closed; most adults started looking for me along with children that were allowed outside – but most were told to stay at home in these early stages with no real answers as to who or why. People split up when searching so they could cover as much ground as possible; the police were also present and soon they were discussing whether to bring the sniffer dogs in to help – that's when I really started to worry about The Lady. Whispers in the village spread fast, even the walls have ears.

After being blamed by both the headmaster and my parents for putting ideas in my head, Mrs Angel became incredibly concerned – she wasn't used to carrying such false guilt. But what was strange was that she was one of the only adults not outside looking for me. Did she secretly hate me and want something bad to happen to me? Was it all a front – to pretend she cared?

She kept herself in the kitchen at home most of the time, drinking endless sugary cups of tea, looking out of her window onto the busy street, watching people search for me; she wasn't relaxed though, she was a jittery mess – you could say she looked guilty … and it was only a matter of time before the police would start to make local arrests, no matter what the whispers were of The Goblin Lady being responsible.

Meanwhile … Kevin – oh the delightful Kevin – had gathered together his usual crowd of naughty boys and girls, about seven of them in total, to go looking for me – but not to find me in one piece, rather to play the game – *who ever found the most missing pieces of me would win a week's supply of chocolate*; no doubt that he would have taken that chocolate from the other children's lunch boxes anyway, same old story.

Kevin's gang were children that didn't really do as they were told; they weren't exactly going to stay indoors during such excitement, even if some of the naughty kids didn't agree with Kevin's horrible games – they were just too scared not to play them with him! You could tell – no matter how important it was to uphold their popular/naughty kid status, most of these children did want to find me in ONE piece! They weren't all bad kids, just felt like they had a reputation to uphold. They were in the woods with slingshots, causing more grief than help; firing rocks at the adults who were looking for me – Kevin's gang were just causing a nuisance.

To ride a badger, or not to ride a badger? That is the badger question.

After a few hours, four cans of coke, three bags of crisps and a go on Tetris to calm my nerves, I decided it was time to announce myself back into the village, to stop them from finding The Lady and potentially hurting her. Against all my will I knew this was a catch twenty-two – as my discovery would mean the bulldozers would begin their destruction and The Lady would once again be unsafe, but I knew she was ready to fight. I knew that she had more of a chance this way: people realising she was innocent rather than her being ransacked by lots of angry strangers – that was a horrible thought, visions of pitchforks and burning torches, she didn't deserve that.

I had to put faith in her plans – not just her plans but the plans of highly skilled badgers it seemed!

And just as I had that thought – in that very moment, Lacey screamed "Badgers!"

"What?" I said.

Lacey went white and froze to the spot. "Henry do you have a pet badger? Two pet badgers actually?"

"No why would I have … jeeez, badgers!!" shouted Henry.

"Oh blimey," I replied, "what are you doing here?"

"Wait you know them?" whispered Lacey.

"Well … kind of?"

"What do you mean kind of? And why are they in my house and wearing those outfits?" said Henry, "Ewww they stink of –"

"Badger's bum and fresh green leaves? Yeah I know." I said.

Both Henry and Lacey were frozen to the spot – this was an intensely weird situation for them, but the past twenty-four hours had already introduced me into this bizarre world – being so close to clothed wildlife – so naturally I took the lead on this one …

I hadn't learned much whilst being in the cabin with The Lady – with regards to animal communication – but I learned enough to realise, right now, the badgers were asking us to come with them. I could also sense The Lady was in trouble, she needed our help, why else would they have sniffed us out?

With panic in the badger's eyes and waving of their heads – they were asking us to come with them – Henry and Lacey were reluctant … which was understandable. Initially I thought both badgers were asking us to come with them when they were swaying their heads, but one of them was actually trying to loosen a scroll from its collar! Yes … that's right – they were wearing the most adorable collars, maybe once lost in the woods by dogs? Now worn by the badgers. Or … were these yet more wonderfully crafted accessories made by The Lady!?

I opened the scroll and it was a letter from The Lady …

I had been mistakenly identified and the search had been called off! Someone had impatiently decided – a simple likeness to myself was apparently enough evidence – I was safe and sound; the green flag had been waved and the bulldozers were on their way in. It was as if time was money and more important than a missing child!

The Lady had assessed the position of the bulldozers, how many workers there were, and timescales. Based on this information, and despite the badgers' disapproval, she had gone for plan number ninety-four, named – *The Saviour of our Mother Lands.* Can you believe they named every plan!?

The animal troops were briefed and ready for action.

Squirrels took to high branches in the tree tops, north east of the woods, loaded with hazelnut launchers, telescopes and bandanas. Foxes wore army camouflage, had announcement whistles and backpacks full of honeycomb containing sleeping bees. The foxes were roaming the lower ground centrally and north …

… You're still thinking about the sleeping bees aren't you …?

Well, the foxes had a certain knack for lullabies which seemed to make bees sleepy: it's an ancient whisper, and one I can confirm is true.

The mice travelled around in roller skates – each like their own little combat vehicle. They wore old school airplane pilot hats and goggles. Their weapon of choice was silly string attached to the front of their roller skate/combat vehicle. The mice were prepped and loaded at the top of mounds. The badgers were like war horses; they would carry and attend to the injured. They could also bash into things with immense force and be that solid base needed in battle. They wore face paint and carried battle horns to announce progress stages in plans – they were very good at organising; they had troops evenly scattered throughout the woodland.

The birds were our planes; they had been creating their very own *special blend* to drop from a height onto the enemy: it consisted of bird poop, badger dribble, fox snot and weasel laughing tears. Talking of weasels … these jester-like creatures were hilariously strange and would pop up behind trees giggling intensely at the enemy to distract them – once the enemy saw them, the weasels would once again hide. They wore the most adorable yellow and red propeller hats – they looked very naughty.

The rabbits took their idea from the bulldozers by attaching a bulldozer type plate to their back legs so they could kick dirt into the enemies eyes; they were hiding ready to ambush centrally, making their way out of the woods from all directions.

The hedgehogs had been practicing a unique type of hedgehog yoga and gymnastics for months, which enabled them to *combine as one* – to create a huge mass of rolling spikes! It was a dangerous ambition, one The Lady really didn't approve of – but a final resort should the bulldozers become too hard to stop; they would wait in the wings for their moment … should they be needed …

And finally, the deer; they were naturally very nervous and although they didn't speak often to The Lady, a mutual respect was had. They heard about the news and offered their support;

they weren't in the original plans as it was felt they couldn't be relied upon due to their flighty nature – but we knew they were there for us.

Wow! – I just said us! That's right; it was us as well now – Lacey, Henry and me. We soon set off riding the badgers into the woods – after I finally convinced them both that The Lady, the animals and the future of Lakeside Hills woodland now also relied on us being a part of the battle too. It seems I met The Lady at just the right time; they needed us now more than ever.

Misty Hill

My parents had heard the news I had been found; they were waiting at home patiently for my return – drinking tea with two police officers. They had no idea that I had been incorrectly identified. I felt relief in the fact they were at peace … temporarily … thinking I was safe; but I couldn't take the risk of returning home to show them I really was safe. I knew they would keep me there, question me, and I would never be able to help The Lady – my true quest.

As we zipped through gardens on badger back, unavoidably ruining everyone's washing lines and mixing clothes up from garden to garden, jumping fence after fence, Mrs Angel managed to catch a glimpse of us from her window. I saw her from the corner of my eye as we passed through her garden – this had prompted her to pack a bag and make her own way to the woods; she just knew that's where we were heading – but I wasn't sure what she was thinking? As I said before, she had been treating this whole ordeal very differently to every other adult. Curiosity as to what on earth must be going on? Did she know all along I would be safe? She was acting so mysteriously, just so different to everyone else.

Kevin and his gang meanwhile were causing more and more mischief; they were having their own catapult fight with the squirrels! They found it hilarious yet slightly freaky that this was actually happening. They didn't quite expect that – when they launched their first catapult at a squirrel – the squirrel would respond by firing hazelnuts back; but it did!

The mice soon realised these naughty children were jeopardising our squirrels' hazelnut resources and came to the rescue! – bouncing over a small mound in the woods – around one hundred mice in their roller skate/combat vehicles, each came crashing towards the children shooting silly string in sync. The children were overwhelmed by the amount of foam and became blinded by the silly string – so had to retreat quickly before they were drowning in the silly stuff! Turning around, the children ran, several running into tree trunks and falling – weeping tears of confusion; they eventually settled together about fifty yards away, taking cover behind a small drop protected by foliage.

"What was that?" cried Kevin.
"M M M Mice on skates?" stuttered one of his stooges.
"What's going on? Why are the animals like … like us? I'm telling my dad – he'll get them; he's won hunter of the year so many times, he'll know what to do." said Kevin.

The naughty kids all set off in pursuit of what was a far worse enemy for the animals, a heartless hunter, an unkind soul: Kevin's mean father – let's just say the apple doesn't fall far from the tree.

Meanwhile … the squirrels gave the mice a thumbs up. That assault was over. Time to return to the master plan – *The Saviour of our Mother Lands*.

The badgers, Lacey, Henry and I found our way through the woods and back to the bunker in super quick time. When we entered it was silent, there was no one there. We wondered where The Lady had gone. We could hear in the distance what sounded like a loud crash of thunder … and again … and again – it echoed through the woods. It was the bulldozers! They had begun their destruction – slowly but surely, they would rip their way through these sorry woods.

As we ran into the furthest room in the bunker to take a look at the plans to grasp an understanding of what to do – that's when we heard her; the most intense and captivating sound! She was standing on Misty Hill overlooking Lakeside Woods – the biggest hill in Lakeside. Her face covered in battle paint, she was wearing a large robe and hood she had made especially for this moment which resembled that of a wizard's cloak; it was thick and an earthy brown colour.

The Lady had carved her very own horn which she used to let all the animals know – the battle had begun! This was the sound that drew our attention away from the cabin. Workers watched from afar, gazing up at Misty Hill through the tall trees on the outskirts of the woodland. "Who is that?" their confused expressions asked.

Soon after The Lady blew her last battle horn instruction – there was a moment of absolute silence.

The bulldozers engines were switched off as everybody tried to work out what was going on. There was an air of anticipation; and the workers felt as though they were being watched. It was an eerie silence – the feeling of calm before the storm. Suddenly a nut was tossed from a tree, hitting one of the workers' helmets! The clack of the nut hitting the helmet echoed, breaking the deathly silence temporarily.

"Did that squirrel just lob a nut at your head Bob?"
"Don't be daft …"
"No it did, seriously."

Suddenly another three nuts hit Bob's helmet.

Both workers looked at the each other, and then look up into the trees. "What on earth?" they said in sync, as a cheeky squirrel giggled and smiled back at them whilst juggling hazelnuts.

Finally, from the top of Misty Hill – The Lady squealed through her battle horn – loud enough to descend across the whole woodland "CHARGE!"

The bulldozers started their engines and moved forwards. The animals charged towards the bulldozers! It was like two huge waves colliding. The Lady was now cantering back down Misty Hill, riding a deer, waving her cane in the air! Various horns and whistles echoed throughout the woodland and village. People who had been evacuated from the woods in order for the demolition to begin – since my incorrect identification – turned to peer back through the trees, trying to make sense of the new commotion.

Mrs Angel had made her way to The Lady's bunker. We had left the bunker by now; we were once again riding the badgers and had set off to meet The Lady. Mrs Angel had somehow found the bunker – we didn't know how? No one else apart from me had ever managed to find it, but she knew exactly where it was. Placing a dust mask over her face, she carefully and intriguingly made her way – looking through beautifully crafted wooden drawers and cupboards – until she found what she seemed to have been looking for: an old photo album. She looked at it for a while … then held it to her chest – a tear rolling down her cheek.

What had she found? What was in the album that brought her to tears?

She took a small picture from her own pocket and placed it in the album. She then put the album back – took a deep breath and left the bunker.

Back at Kevin's house, Kevin had explained to his dad the strange events they had encountered. Kevin's dad was called Phil – he was a huge man; he wore an ill-fitting tank top which didn't cover his entire gut, dirty jeans and a filthy cap which read 'Mississippi Hunting Tour 57' which must have been some old hunting merchandise from the U.S.A.

"You think I'm going back out there, boy? That scrawny Neverstump lad has been found; we're not needed anymore – not unless you're going to tell me you found a tasty herd of deer I can hunt?"

"Not exactly … umm squirrels and rabbits dad?"

"Ha! I gave up hunting pathetic roadkill when I was younger than you! Now take your little gang of friends and get out of here, and grab me a beer on the way out."

"But they had … they aren't normal dad – they had weapons."

"Who did?"

"The animals, they attacked us!"

"Get out of here, stop telling porkies."

"They did sir, look!" said one of Kevin's friends – showing a graze and some cuts from their brief encounter with the squirrels.

"You kids are pulling my leg, aren't you?" They all responded showing their injuries individually.

"Animals with weapons huh? I bet you think I was born yesterday. If it was just you boy I would be grounding you right now for a week, but as your friends are backing this story up I'll give you the benefit of the doubt … but I assure you, if you're lying, you're grounded for TWO weeks."

"I'm not Dad, I promise."

"Fine, get my hunting gear…"

Captain Bobby Langford

We finally caught up with The Lady at the bottom of Misty Hill; she was out of breath and back to her scatty self –
"We must save the woodland! Save the woodland from these dirty rich … wait – I was going to say dirty rich pigs, but I quite like pigs, and that's an insult to pigs." said The Lady.

She started muttering to herself for a good few moments about what word she could add on to the end of rich and dirty. She got lost in that moment temporarily … meanwhile, we were just standing there watching her deep in thought to herself. In the background you could see engine smoke and fumes coming from the woods; the sounds of unwelcome man-made machines, animals, battle horns and whistles. It was as if the woodland had come alive with a concoction of contradiction – so alive yet fighting for its last breath in its final moments of truth. The devil was now, well and truly, knocking at nature's door.

"Margaret!" I shouted – to snap her out of her daze – "Does it really matter?"

"No, I guess it really doesn't? Right, gather round, this is what we do." She held out a large sheet with plans on.

"As we speak, the birds are dropping Gross-Bombs on the heads of the workers to distract them. The weasels have climbed up inside the engines and started to chew the wires. The badgers are knocking down all the chemical toilets; it may smell down there but it's giving those horrible people another reason to leave. What we need to do is make our way to the cabin where they have a computer and scan and send this story to the local newspaper; let me explain – since I found out about the development plans, I have read every history book on Lakeside Woods I could get my grubby grabbers on – to find any reason to stop this from happening. A few days ago, I came across something quite magnificent – the story of Captain Bobby Langford: a soldier from a civil war in 1610, who, along with the king, dedicated a small part of the woods as a memorial site. Well … I dug that small site up, a site lost for hundreds of years beneath soil and stone! I found it: a way to save the woodland. It's to the south; the bulldozers are far away but we must hurry – this news must be spread, it's our only chance!"

Kevin's dad Phil had made his way to the woods; his small tribe following closely behind. He was dressed in his hunting gear which included a flare and baton. As they began to venture deeper into the woods, the weasels started giggling from behind the trees. Phil was looking around in a panic – it wasn't something he had experienced before. As the laughter grew louder and the closer, he began to get dizzy as the onset of confusion and anxiety took over. He felt as though his head was spinning – the panic and disorientation forced him to start running further into the forest – the children blindly following him. As a last resort he blasted his flare into the air uncontrollably, letting off a bright red light. Birds flapped and animals yelped … he didn't shoot anything, it was just a warning to stop them toying with him. There was a brief silence – everyone across the woodland heard and saw the flare, and stood still momentarily; it sparked new panic. Why was there someone with a flare in the woods?

Suddenly a large net scooped up all the kids that were following behind Phil and held them high in the trees; the contraption broke the silence. It was a net trap The Lady had set earlier that day – the children screamed!

"Dad what's happening?"
Phil stopped and stared for a moment, trying to take in what had just happened.
"Do you know what – you're better off up there; I'll come back for you all later. There are some strange things going on down here and I want to get to the bottom of it without any more distractions …"
"But I'm hungry!"
"You're always hungry! Why are you thinking about food now?"
Phil started walking off deeper into the woods …
"Dad? Dad?" Kevin shouted in a panic.
"I don't think he's coming back," said one of the other children to Kevin. All the children peered through the tiny squares in the netting, nervously holding on tight, watching Phil walk deeper into the woods.

The Lady, Lacey, Henry and I had advanced towards the workers' cabin; we needed to distract the management from inside – somehow get them to come out! They were already distracted by the flare; many of the workers were looking out of the cabin windows. It was going to take something extraordinary to make them leave the cabin.

First, Lacey pretended she was lost and scared – so walked towards the cabin crying. This gave Henry the opportunity to sneak closer. As Henry was the computer whiz, we knew he would be the one to crack the computer system, should we get the opportunity … Lacey's cries were enough to distract the workers away from the cabin to see to her … until she heard a voice …

"Lacey? What are you doing here?"

"Uncle Tom!?" she replied shocked.

Her Uncle Tom was one of the workers! She hadn't even realised.

"You know her Tom?" a worker asked.

"Yeah that's my Lacey. Come on let's get you home young lady, you shouldn't be out here."

Lacey made a bit more fuss, making things difficult for Uncle Tom; this was just a tactic to distract the workers from seeing Henry enter the Cabin. Lacey's efforts weren't enough – now Uncle Tom could take over and handle Lacey alone, the workers started heading back towards the cabin. That's when The Lady took drastic action – a vision imprinted on many workers'/victims' brains forever …

"Look away!" she said to me.

"What?" I replied confused.

"Look away! Now! You have to – to save Henry" she said in a panic.

In that moment I didn't want to do anything to ruin the plans, so I did as I was told. I didn't see what happened but have since learned – she ran up to the cabin as the workers were walking back inside, and lifted up her robe to reveal a scrawny, hairy and wrinkly body. I had never heard men scream and run like that before – even to this day, those screams still haunt me. She didn't just clear the cabin; she cleared everyone within one hundred yards … we were in!

As Kevin's dad Phil was making his way down a steep ridge, he heard the laughter of weasels again; this started to really mess with his head – "SHUT UP!" he shouted. "Leave me alone!" Spinning around anxiously trying to locate the little jesters …

In his moment of disorientation, he saw foxes dressed in camouflage at the bottom of the hill. He stood looking at them for a brief moment – double vision and squinting his eyes, trying to figure out if what he saw was real. He then grabbed a baton from his rucksack and ran towards them … the foxes then reached into their backpacks and grabbed the honeycombs containing sleeping bees. They tossed the honeycombs into the air, landing halfway up the ridge – Phil stopped in his path, slipping in the process. He looked closer at the honeycomb, trying to work out why they had been thrown. Suddenly he heard a *Buzzzzz!* "No … no! Not bees, I'm allergic! No, please!" Phil cried.

Hundreds of angry bees awoke from their slumber; blaming Phil for the rude awakening! Phil tried desperately to scramble back up the slippery, muddy ridge … a sweaty, dribbling mess of a man was quickly being reduced from hunter to the hunted. In his pitiful attempt to climb the ridge, his overweight and unfit frame slipped and fell all the way to the bottom, aggravating yet more bees on the way down! By now the foxes were long gone. Phil ran off screaming, jumping, scratching and slapping himself – deeper into the woods; a swarm of angry bees followed not far behind.

Since the bulldozers to the north side of the woods had been abandoned and tampered with; more had been ordered to the south side of the woods – creating panic that the memorial would be ruined before they had a chance to save it. The Lady left Henry and me to try and hack the computers and send through the vital information to the local newspaper. The Lady made her way across to the other side of the woods on deer-back after her trusty winged advisors told her news of the new bulldozers arriving. The news spread quickly, and hundreds of badgers diverted to the south. Using all their strength, the badgers charged and pushed back against the bulldozers, but they were really struggling – can you even begin to imagine how hard that must have been for the poor badgers? The workers were so confused by the animals' actions. Some of the workers started to feel rather uncomfortable after they ended up inevitably hurting and injuring the animals that stood in their way; but they carried on; they had a job to do and a lack of compassion meant many workers enjoyed the fight rather than trying to understand why this miracle was happening.

As the Lady was making her way across the woods on deer-back – she felt a rope lasso around her waist; the deer kept running, but the rope was tightly bound around her, pulling her to the floor! She landed with a THUMP!

Dazed and confused, she regained her consciousness to find herself tied to a tree staring at that horrible man, Kevin's dad – Phil! Phil wasn't in the best condition – he had around twenty large, red, puss-filled stings on his arms, neck and face. His lips and tongue had swollen to around twice the size due to an allergic reaction. This caused him to speak funnily with a heavy lisp. You could still just about make out what he was saying, but The

Lady certainly took advantage and made fun where she could.

"Look what I've got here then, so it's true what they say – The Goblin Lady does exist: you are ugly!"

"You aren't too pretty yourself! Let yourself go a bit, haven't you?" she replied.

"Shut up!! I'm a work in progress." he said, seemingly insulted.

"Now that ..." as she pointed "is most definitely a finished article I'm afraid; even if you have tried some of that fashionable cosmetic surgery – lip filler is it?"

"Beeeeees" he said, spitting through a lisp, struggling to cope with his new mouth abnormalities.

"Come again?" she replied. She knew what he was saying but took advantage and played games with him.

"Bees" he spat.

"Again?"

"Bees" his frustration grew, to her amusement.

"Again?"

This went on for much longer than you would expect …

"Right! Enough from you; what's going on around here? I'm looking to buy one of these new houses once they're built and there's some weird things happening – animals are fighting back?"

"Too right they are – and we won't let this go ahead."

"What do you mean? You're a part of this madness too? What have you done to the animals? Why are they behaving this way? I don't like it one bit, it's not normal."

"Who are you to decide how they should behave? They have as much right to live here as you do – if not more, you worthless slob."

"Well I'm keeping you here until half of that woodland is obliterated." said Phil. The Lady was horrified.

"But you can't? I need … I have to … please don't do this, please."

Phil sat on the ground next to her with a smug grin on his face. He grabbed a beer from his bag and sipped it slowly.

Henry and I saw workers coming back; they must have realised The Lady had gone. We struggled – but eventually managed to email across the article to the newspaper; all we could do now was wait; but that felt useless as the woodland and the memorial would continue to be destroyed until the news was received. As we tried to leave the cabin, we got caught and pulled out by our ears with a severe telling off – but they had no idea we had managed to access their computer. Just as we thought we couldn't escape, and our parents would be notified, two badgers appeared at full speed from nowhere picking us up and throwing us on their backs! We were off again – and to the south we went! The workers were left open mouthed, scratching their heads.

To the south!

Lacey had managed to sneak her way back out of the house undetected, once her uncle dropped her off. She had been making her way through the woods when she heard cries from above; as she looked up it was Kevin and his friends! Lacey stood, arms folded – looking at them whilst smiling.

"Oh dear oh dear: it's Kevin and his pack of strays."

"Lacey get us down! Please! Adam keeps farting."

"No I don't!" protested Adam.

"Well someone is, it stinks up here."

"No … I think I'll leave you a little longer; how did you get up there anyway?"

"I don't know! It just happened. Lacey the animals are … they're dangerous! Don't leave us here."

"They're only dangerous if you're mean to them – are you being mean? Again?"

"Not exactly no. Anyway, my dad's going to get them all now."

"Your dad? As in … the hunter?"

"Heard of him then have you?" Kevin said, all smug.

"Only because my daddy says he's a bully! He only acts tough when he has his hunting gear in his hands; which way did he go?"

"I'll tell you if you let us down."

"No you tell me first."

"Ok … ok – he went that way …" Kevin pointed deeper into the woods.

"Thanks!" Lacey ran off into the distance; she didn't even look back!

"Lacey? You promised!" Kevin shouted.

The naughty children were once again left hanging in the large net.

"Who just farted again? Aww it stinks … LET US DOWN!" Kevin screamed.

After visiting The Lady's bunker, Mrs Angel made her way deeper into the woods. A kindness oozed from Mrs Angel and meant the animals felt attached to her; they trusted her. She was mesmerised by the tiny birds that were flying near her head – chirping happily! There were also rodents walking besides her feet – tickling and rubbing against her bare ankles.

"Oh my… what are you darlings doing? This is so strange. Where are you trying to lead me?"

They started to pull her in a new direction; it felt unkind to pull back against them, so she naturally let them lead her. Suddenly Lacey came bursting through the bushes and bumped right into Mrs Angel's chest. The animals disbursed quickly in a panic.

"Oh Lacey! Where have you come from? Calm down will you!" Lacey was out of breath and in a hurry.
"We've got to save them; we've got to help them!"
"Save who?"
"The Lady, the animals, Ivor and Henry … the woods, everything!"
"Wow, I don't know where to start. Are they ok? Is anyone hurt?"
"We have to be quicker!" Lacey pulled at Mrs Angel's sleeve.
"But the animals were guiding me; I know that sounds weird but –"
"No it's not weird; we should listen to them." Said Lacey enthusiastically.
"Ok …"

They both asked the animals to return after the brief commotion – and they did. The animals then began to guide Mrs Angel and Lacey; but where they were guiding them – they weren't entirely sure. They knew to trust the animals' judgement; it just felt right.

As Henry and I approached the south side of the woods, we could see the destruction already happening, even from afar. The bulldozers must have been only one hundred yards from the memorial site which was our only hope to stop all of this from happening; we must protect the memorial site!

We decided to split; we knew *now* that the animals would listen to us – even if we didn't fully understand them back. I decided to go to the memorial site, whilst Henry would be at the far south side to create as much of a distraction as he could. The badgers and I were now pulling fallen trees from the south to the memorial, in an attempt to create a large tree stump barricade to protect the memorial site as best as we could until the bulldozers got close. This felt like a last-ditch attempt to protect our only hope.

The battle I heard about – to the far south – was like something of nightmares; I'll never forget what Henry relayed to me after, utter carnage. Things I feel uncomfortable relaying to you, even now. You finally felt the affect this had on the wildlife; they knew that if their homes got torn down, they may never find another. And then it wouldn't be too long until their lives were over, without their precious home, they wouldn't be able to live safely.

Squirrels were carrying other small injured friends on mini stretchers across the ground to safety. Birds were tired; there was nowhere safe for them to land anymore – they were falling out of the sky; they would rather *fight and fall* for their trees and friends, than *abandon and fly* to another home. The birds – more so than any other animal – could start a new life as travel was so easy; but they never gave up on their fellow land dwellers; they would fight until the very end. Foxes were consoling weasels, who no longer had the heart to laugh – they were crying and shaking. Mice had all but lost their skates – the wheels had become buckled or broken; they were working tirelessly like mechanics but felt they were falling behind.

And Henry – god bless him – was like a captain, trying to hold them all together.

But the bulldozers kept coming … and despite the animals' struggles … those that were still able, would continue to fight for their woodland – so long as they could still stand.

As Mrs Angel and Lacey walked through the woods – being led by their new-found animal buddies – they heard voices in the distance. They crept slowly and closer … to find it was The Lady tied up, with Kevin's dad – Phil – sitting on the ground next to her. Mrs Angel was a pretty lady; it was of no surprise that Phil fancied her. He'd made a pass at her before, but she'd brushed off his advances. Mrs Angel thought he was quite a repulsive character. She decided to distract Phil with her charm.

"Who goes there?" shouted Phil.
"Hello stranger; what are you up to here then? This doesn't look fair?"

The Lady and Mrs Angel locked eyes but kept quiet. The Lady was shocked to see her – like a ghost – but she wasn't scared. Phil had taken his hat off and held it to his chest like a naughty little boy; he stood up and faced her.

"What … what are you doing here?" he stuttered.
"I could ask you the same thing?"
"We were … I was just … you know … she's …" Phil kept bumbling on.
"What happened to you?" said Mrs Angel.
"You can hardly speak!?"
Just before Phil said bees – he looked at The Lady, remembering how she teased him last time, so changed his answer.

"I'm allergic – I got stung – a lot!" Phil said, as a final bee flew out of his hat and stung his cheek. Phil screamed and threw his hat. He tried to stand brave – trying to impress and show no fear – but he was now really struggling with his allergy and the pain.

"Don't you think you should go to hospital?" said Mrs Angel.
"No I'm … I'm fine." Phil replied unconvincingly.
"Well then don't you think you should let her go?"

"I can't." he said as he changed the tone of his voice.

"Why? What has she done to deserve such treatment?"

"You wouldn't understand; honestly – it's for the best though."

As the conversation kept going around in circles – her asking, and him not answering correctly – Lacey snuck behind them and untied The Lady! They made a dart for it, deep into the woods. Mrs Angel kept Phil bumbling for as long as possible until he turned around to realise what had happened.

"You sneaky little …" Phil said as he walked towards her.

"Woah, no closer; what are you thinking?" she said.

"Well I've got some spare rope, and I don't trust you as much as I don't trust that Goblin Lady freak."

"You shouldn't call her that …"

"Why? Why do you care?"

"I think you'll find they disagree with you as well …"

"Who?"

"Them!" Mrs Angel said as she pointed up into the trees. There were around fifty squirrels loaded with nuts ready to launch; they were all giggling. Mrs Angel made a dash for it, and – just as Phil was about to follow – hundreds of nuts came flying through the air, knocking him down and out for the count!

Her legacy

I had finally – with the majority of help from the badgers – managed to build a large secure log wall around the memorial. A bulldozer was getting closer … and closer; crashing through smaller trees and foliage. Its engine so loud; thrashing like thunder!

Finally, the bulldozer reached the wall. The driver got out to assess the strange *log wall* he didn't expect to see there. This wall wasn't in the planning map he thought – taking a sneak peek through a gap in the log wall. He looked back at his co-driver, shook his head in confusion and told him to carry on – "Knock it down," he shouted, "drive straight through it."

I was hiding and in a real panic so decided to do something drastic. I told the badgers I would put myself in danger and stand in front the bulldozer to try and stop them! Just as I left to do so, I heard barking in the distance. Who was it, I thought? I looked up to see Mr Albert ˉᵔusage! He was being led through the woods

by a bird carrying a large sack of hotdogs;
Albert was chasing the bird with the hotdogs.
But this wasn't any coincidence; this smart bird
knew exactly what it was doing! This bird had
a plan.

The bird dropped all the hotdogs inside the
workers large boots and Albert began biting
their ankles! Both workers started running
around yelping, demanding Albert stop. I took
this opportunity to grab the keys from the
ignition and threw them as far as I could. With
the woodland so vast in foliage – they wouldn't
find the keys even if they tried. But it wasn't
enough; two more bulldozers came crashing
towards us – three – then four! We were
powerless.

The hedgehogs knew they had a job to do;
something they had practiced for months – to
join together to create a huge spikey ball; big
enough to stop ten bulldozers. But they just
couldn't do it! They were struggling to connect.
Every time they tried, they would all fall to the
ground in a large heap of hedgehogs. They
didn't give up! But time was now running out;

and they were becoming increasingly scared and vulnerable, individually.

Henry had all but lost his battle on the very south side of the woods; the bulldozers had all now passed through. Henry was left helping injured and upset animals. He knew there was no more he could do to help me at the memorial, so he stayed with the animals, collecting them together – with the help of other animals still able – and began taking them back to the cabin, where he could at least try to treat them using the medical supplies available.

Four huge bulldozers were now only meters away from crashing through the log barrier we had created. The Lady and Lacey had finally made it to the south side; they froze in horror at what they were about to see … the life and soul of Lakeside being ripped apart and gone forever; their precious woodland being destroyed.

The Lady grabbed Lacey and told her to stand back and take cover – Lacey asked why. The Lady explained there was no time to discuss – *just do as I say now!*

The Lady crouched down into a ball – curled up real tight; she looked useless – as though she was a shy hedgehog hiding from the danger. All of a sudden, the forest started to shake, and bright lights appeared from The Lady like rays of sunshine! It was a beautiful and enchanting sight.

Slowly she rose to her feet, stretched out her arms – as though she was letting off an energy – so powerful, you could only stop and stare in awe – open-mouthed.

Leaves started swirling in their thousands creating tornados; the trees were swaying; workers lost their hats but they didn't care – they were fixated on this new phenomenon all around them. Suddenly hundreds – maybe thousands! – of hedgehogs started rising into sky, as if they were being levitated by a magical power. Slowly and carefully they started sticking together to create what looked like a Ferris-Wheel from a fun fair; but this wheel was huge, spikey and hedgehoggy!

Fully formed, the wheel then started to roll slowly; it creaked as it moved as if it was an old part not oiled for years. It soon picked up momentum and headed right for the bulldozers – workers ran for their lives; screaming and jumping from the seats of their vehicles. The giant wheel picked up high speed and crashed straight through four huge bulldozers – completely flattening them like pancakes! Terrified workers ran back to the far south-side cabin to tell the management of the horror they just witnessed; most had already been aware of what felt like a mini earthquake from afar.

The Lady began to fall back as though the life had been completely sucked out of her; but as she fell, she was caught by Mrs Angel. Mrs Angel fell to her knees – as The Lady lay lifeless in her arms. For a moment the world stopped still. The woods were completely and consistently silent for the first time in decades – you could sense something epic had just happened.

It was as if every sentient being had stopped and held their breath for The Lady, as she struggled to find hers.

We all stood watching … I had Albert Sausage in my arms – I never wanted to let him go again. Lacey came and held my hand; we smiled at each other – it was the first time I really felt that connection. As I told you before, I did adore her.

Henry was also now with us; battered and bruised like a true soldier.

No sign of Kevin, his friends or his dad … maybe the weasels had them now … or the bees …

Some vehicles had pulled up; we could hear and see them through the trees to the far south side of the woods. It was the police and the newspaper company – they had got the message! Although it was us that temporarily stopped the bulldozers; the police finalised the operation by shutting everything down. They taped off the memorial site to protect it and could now act upon the forgotten discovery.

The Lady slowly looked up at Mrs Angel – a tear rolled down both their cheeks.
"Did we do it?" The Lady asked?

"You did it, Margaret," Mrs Angel replied.
"Will they leave us now Laura? Will they leave us in peace?" The Lady said to Mrs Angel.
"I think so. You're a good person; mum would have been so proud of you. No matter what people think – you *DO* what you love. You truly follow your heart like no one I've ever known; and I wish we hadn't drifted apart over the years."
"*DID* – what I love …" said Margaret (The Lady).
"What do you mean – *did*?" replied Laura (Mrs Angel).
"I'm too tired … I'm too weak. What just happened – It wasn't normal, and I know that. But I have nothing left inside – just remember *Mother Nature* was here …" said Margaret struggling to speak.

Margaret started to close her eyes and lose consciousness. Laura started to cry and shout "Someone call an ambulance – I'm losing her …"
After that everything became a blur; it was far too upsetting – like slow motion. We were just running around doing whatever we could to help, but the The Lady was slipping away. It

wasn't long before we heard new sirens – but not police sirens this time – an ambulance had arrived. There was nothing more we could do; we all went home.

Twelve weeks later, and Mrs Angel had been absent all that time, so we were stuck with a supply teacher. A big meany-pants called Mr Rogers! We really did miss Mrs Angel.

We assumed she was initially absent to mourn for her sister – The Lady. But time went by and we still hadn't seen her, so I decided to make my way to the bunker – it was to be the first time I had returned since the day I went missing.

I decided this time I probably shouldn't make the same journey alone, so I asked Lacey and Henry to come with me. When we reached the bunker we all looked at each other in anticipation before we knocked – just as I raised my hand to knock, the door creaked open … and there stood Mrs Angel – but a dishevelled thinner version; bird poop in her hair, tiny sticks in her teeth and mud on her face.

Despite all that, she had the biggest grin on her face! She was just so happy to carry on her sister's legacy.

"Come in." she said. "I knew you would return; we all did!" The familiar faces of the animals we saved surrounded her and they all waved to us in unison.

Some people say, even to this very day –
Mother Nature, in one form or another, still
lives in those woods ... I guess you'll just have
to find out for yourselves ...

The End.